Welcome to ALADDIN QUIX!

If you are looking for fast, fun-to-read stories with colorful characters, lots of kid-friendly humor, easy-to-follow action, entertaining story lines, and lively illustrations, then **ALADDIN QUIX** is for you!

But wait, there's more!

If you're also looking for stories with tables of contents; word lists; about-the-book questions; 64, 80, or 96 pages; short chapters; short paragraphs; and large fonts, then **ALADDIN QUIX** is *definitely* for you!

ALADDIN QUIX: The next step between ready to reads and longer, more challenging chapter books, for readers five to eight years old.

Gondola to Danger

Read all the ALADDIN QUIX books!

By Stephanie Calmenson

Our Principal Is a Frog!
Our Principal Is a Wolf!
Our Principal's in His Underwear!

Royal Sweets
By Helen Perelman

Book 1: *A Royal Rescue*
Book 2: *Sugar Secrets*
Book 3: *Stolen Jewels*

A Miss Mallard Mystery
By Robert Quackenbush

Dig to Disaster
Texas Trail to Calamity
Express Train to Trouble
Stairway to Doom
Bicycle to Treachery
Gondola to Danger

A Miss Mallard Mystery

GONDOLA TO
DANGER

EL
DUCKO

ROBERT QUACKENBUSH

ALADDIN QUIX

New York   London   Toronto   Sydney   New Delhi

This book is a work of fiction. Any references to historical events, real people, or real places are used fictitiously. Other names, characters, places, and events are products of the author's imagination, and any resemblance to actual events or places or persons, living or dead, is entirely coincidental.

ALADDIN QUIX

Simon & Schuster Children's Publishing Division

1230 Avenue of the Americas, New York, New York 10020

This Aladdin QUIX paperback edition January 2019

Copyright © 1983 by Robert Quackenbush

Also available in an Aladdin QUIX hardcover edition.

All rights reserved, including the right of reproduction in whole or in part in any form.

ALADDIN and the related marks and colophon are trademarks of Simon & Schuster, Inc.

For information about special discounts for bulk purchases, please contact Simon & Schuster Special Sales at 1-866-506-1949 or business@simonandschuster.com.

The Simon & Schuster Speakers Bureau can bring authors to your live event. For more information or to book an event contact the Simon & Schuster Speakers Bureau at 1-866-248-3049 or visit our website at www.simonspeakers.com.

Designed by Nina Simoneaux

The illustrations for this book were rendered in pen and ink and wash.

The text of this book was set in Archer Medium.

Manufactured in the United States of America 1218 OFF

2 4 6 8 10 9 7 5 3 1

Library of Congress Control Number 2018959531

ISBN 978-1-5344-1406-8 (hc)

ISBN 978-1-5344-1405-1 (pbk)

ISBN 978-1-5344-1407-5 (eBook)

First for Piet and Margie,

and now for Emma and Aidan

Cast of Characters

Miss Mallard: World-famous ducktective

El Ducko: A famous artist

Alfredo: A Doge's Palace guard

Enrico: A Doge's Palace officer

Gino: A gondolier who takes Miss Mallard around Venice's canals

What's in Miss Mallard's Bag?

Miss Mallard has many detective tools she brings with her on her adventures around the world.

In her knitting bag she usually has:

- Newspaper clippings
- Knitting needles and yarn
- A magnifying glass
- A flashlight
- A mirror
- A travel guide
- Chocolates for her nephew

Contents

1

Art Theft!

Miss Mallard, the world-famous ducktective, was at the opera festival in Venice when the Italian police asked for her help. A priceless masterpiece had been stolen from the Doge's Palace.

Miss Mallard hurried across the Piazza San Marco—one of the most beautiful squares in the world—to the entrance of the palace. When she got there, a pigeon handed her a note and said, "A duck wearing a mask told me to give this to you."

Miss Mallard read the note. It said: **"NEVER FEAR, EL DUCKO IS NEAR!"**

"That's nice to know," said Miss Mallard, quacking with delight.

Once inside, Miss Mallard met

the police and palace officers. **Alfredo**, a palace guard, carried Miss Mallard's knitting bag, which contained her detective tools and clipping file.

They all went upstairs to a heavy locked door. Alfredo held the knitting bag **awkwardly** with his right wing. And then he began unlocking the door with his left.

"This is where the theft occurred," said **Enrico**, a palace officer. "We locked the door to

keep tourists out until after your investigation."

"Good thinking!" said Miss Mallard. "When did this happen?"

"Just after we all came on duty," said Enrico. "We are here from ten to six. At ten thirty someone yelled, **'Fire!'** It was a phony alarm. And when we returned, the painting was gone."

The door was unlocked, and everyone went into the room. Miss Mallard looked around and gasped at what she saw!

6

In the empty space where the stolen painting had been hung was a large drawing of a weeping convict. It was signed **"El Ducko"**!

"This is the only clue that was left behind by the thief," said Enrico.

"How can this be?" cried Miss Mallard. "I just learned that El Ducko is in Venice, but he could not have done this. I know him. He saved my life in Madrid. He keeps his identity a secret,

but that doesn't make him a crook. He is a great artist who is **dedicated** to helping others and giving his riches to the poor, not stealing."

"But you can see for yourself that the drawing is definitely an El Ducko," said Enrico. "And when we went to arrest him at his studio, he was gone. **You must find him!**"

"All right," said Miss Mallard. "Let me see the drawing."

Alfredo took down the drawing

and handed it to her. Miss Mallard examined it carefully.

"I'm sure this drawing contains a clue," she said. "I'll take it with me. And I'll return when I know something."

"May I order a **gondola** for you?" asked Alfredo.

"Please," said Miss Mallard.

Alfredo went to the window and motioned to one of the **gondoliers** standing in front of the palace.

"**Gino** is dependable," he said

to Miss Mallard. "He'll be waiting for you downstairs."

Miss Mallard quickly rolled up the drawing and put it in her knitting bag next to the note from El Ducko. When everything was in place, she hurried outside.

2

Gondola Ride

Gino was waiting for Miss Mallard at the front door of the palace.

"A pleasure to meet you, **signora**," Gino said.

He took Miss Mallard to his gondola.

On the way, Miss Mallard unrolled the drawing and asked, "Does this picture remind you of anything, Gino?"

"It is a very sad picture, signora," answered Gino.

"It is sad," said Miss Mallard. "But are there any sad places in this beautiful city? I believe that is what this drawing is about."

"Only the Bridge of Sighs is sad," answered Gino.

He added, "That is where, in olden times, prisoners crossed

the **canal** from the palace to the **dungeon**."

"Take me there!" said Miss Mallard.

"Sì, signora," said Gino. He helped Miss Mallard into his gondola. "I will go as fast as I am able. **Pronto!**"

With his long oar, Gino guided the gondola from one canal to another. It took a long, long, long time.

Finally they came to a dark, narrow passageway.

"This is it," said Gino. "There is the Bridge of Sighs overhead."

"But this is just around the corner from the front entrance to the palace!" said Miss Mallard in surprise.

"But, signora!" Gino **protested**. "I thought you would enjoy the **scenic** route!"

"Oh, Gino," said Miss Mallard. "Take me to the wall over there. I see another drawing taped to it."

Gino did as Miss Mallard asked. Indeed, there was another

drawing, and Miss Mallard pulled it from the wall. It showed melons piled on a table and an **awning** overhead. **It was signed *El Ducko*!**

"There is something about these drawings that makes me think El Ducko did not do them," said Miss Mallard, "but I haven't been able to figure it out. Still, there must be a reason for them."

She turned to Gino and asked, "Where can melons be found in Venice?"

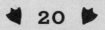

"Everywhere, signora," said Gino.

"Hmmm," said Miss Mallard. "The drawing makes me think of a market. Take me to the biggest market, Gino, and no scenic routes this time, please."

"Pronto, signora," said Gino.

Gino aimed the gondola forward to the Grand Canal. The Rialto Bridge loomed before them. Looking upward, Miss Mallard caught a glimpse of a cloaked figure wearing a mask.

There at the top of the bridge, she was certain that she saw the masked figure peering at her from behind a pillar.

"El Ducko!" she cried.

But as soon as she called, the figure disappeared.

3

Masked Duck

Miss Mallard was puzzled. If that was El Ducko, why was he hiding from her?

Gino pulled on the long oar of his gondola and headed slowly for an entrance to the Rialto Bridge. When they got there, Gino started rowing.

"Walk over the bridge," he said to Miss Mallard. "The market is nearby. I'll wait here for you."

Miss Mallard went right to the market. Sure enough, she found a melon stand like the one in the drawing. She also found another drawing of flying pigeons taped to the side of the stand.

As Miss Mallard left the market, she caught another glimpse of the masked figure. Again she called to him.

But he disappeared in the crowd. Now she was confused. Was El Ducko guilty after all?

Sadly, Miss Mallard went back to the waiting gondola.

"Take me back to the Piazza San Marco where the pigeons gather," she said to Gino. "That's what this new drawing is about, I'm sure."

"Pronto, signora," said Gino.

After yet another very slow gondola ride, Miss Mallard was at last delivered to the great square.

Many tourists were having their

pictures taken with the pigeons. Then two pigeons recognized her and wanted their pictures taken with her.

"Please go away," pleaded Miss Mallard. "I'm on a very important case."

But the pigeons didn't listen.

More and more and more pigeons crowded around her. She couldn't move.

She wondered what to do. She was stuck!

Then a clock bell struck two.

All at once the pigeons flew away.

"Whew," said Miss Mallard with a sigh. "Saved by the old Venetian custom of feeding the pigeons their lunch at two o'clock."

She walked around the square. At the bell tower, she saw another drawing taped to a wall. The new drawing was of an artist's **palette** with the number 1496 written across it. And like all the others, the drawing was signed with the same back-slanted El Ducko signature.

"Something disturbs me about

these drawings," Miss Mallard said to herself. "I wish I could think what it is."

Miss Mallard ran back to Gino.

"This drawing can only mean I should go to the artists' quarter," said Miss Mallard. "Take me there at once."

Then Miss Mallard again caught a glimpse of the masked figure.

"El Ducko!" cried Miss Mallard.

Too late!

He was gone!

Miss Mallard was worried. Why was El Ducko still hiding from her? "That is not like him," she thought.

"Hurry, Gino," said Miss Mallard. "I must find out what this is all about."

4

Wild Duck Chase

But Gino kept his usual pace. Miss Mallard wondered how anyone could be so slow.

They went under a hundred bridges before they at last came to the artists' quarter.

Miss Mallard got out of the gondola and went to knock on the door of number 1496. She saw that it was open.

"Anyone home?" she called.

Hearing no answer, she went inside. She looked around and saw paintings hanging everywhere. She knew at once that she was in El Ducko's studio.

Suddenly, she saw what it was that was different about all the drawings she had found and the paintings in El Ducko's studio.

The signatures were not the same. The signatures on the *paintings* slanted to the *right*. The signatures on the *drawings* slanted to the *left*. **Which were El Ducko's?**

Then Miss Mallard remembered the note the pigeon had handed her in the square. She took it out of her knitting bag. The signature on the note matched the paintings, not the drawings.

At last, this was the proof she needed. She ran outside.

"Take me back to the Doge's

Palace, Gino," she said. "And **please, please hurry**! I must get there before it's too late."

"Pronto, signora," said Gino.

Gino steered his gondola back through the winding canals. But he was even slower than before.

The gondola went through one twisting canal after another. None of them looked familiar to a very worried Miss Mallard.

"Are you sure you are taking me back to the palace, Gino?" she asked. Gino didn't answer.

Suddenly, Miss Mallard knew the truth. She was being delayed by Gino on purpose! It was all a plot to keep her from returning to the palace.

The next bridge they came to, Miss Mallard jumped and grabbed hold of the railing. The gondola tipped with such a **jolt** that Gino fell into the canal before he could grab her. Then someone reached over the railing and pulled Miss Mallard to safety.

5

True Signature

"El Ducko!" cried Miss Mallard with surprise and delight.

"To the rescue," said El Ducko. "I told you I would be near. But I must keep **out of sight** of the police until my name is cleared."

"I *have* cleared your name!" said Miss Mallard. "I don't have time to explain. We must get to the palace at once. If we get there after the clock strikes six, it will be too late. Then everyone will believe that you *did* steal the painting, no matter what I tell them. **Let's hurry!**"

They got to the palace just as the clock in the square struck six. They saw someone leaving the palace with a large package under his wing.

"Stop him, El Ducko!" cried Miss Mallard. "He's got your painting!"

With that, El Ducko leaped and tossed the thief to the ground. The police and palace officers heard the racket and came running!

"**Here is your thief**," said Miss Mallard. "And it is not El Ducko."

"Alfredo, our trusted guard!" cried Enrico, the palace officer.

"Right!" said Miss Mallard. "He set everything up to make it

look as if El Ducko had stolen the painting. He copied El Ducko's work and used the drawings to throw us off the track."

"It was Alfredo who sounded the alarm!" exclaimed Enrico.

"Yes," said Miss Mallard. "And while everyone was away, he hid the painting in the palace. His plan was to take it with him when he got off duty at six. That's why he sent me on a **wild duck chase**, which he also planned in advance, knowing that I would be investigating the case. One of his gang, Gino, was supposed to keep me from coming back to the palace before Alfredo made his getaway."

"How did you figure it out?" snarled Alfredo.

"Because you are left-winged," said Miss Mallard. "I remembered that you unlocked the door with your *left* wing. All the signatures on the drawings slanted to the left, like most left-winged ducks would do.

"This proved to me that El Ducko

did not do them, because he is right-winged," she added. "That is how I knew that you faked the signatures."

"Take him away!" Enrico said to the police. "And find and arrest that phony gondolier, Gino, too."

"Pronto!" said the police.

As the police led him away, Alfredo glared at Miss Mallard.

Enrico turned to thank Miss Mallard and El Ducko, but they were already on their way to

see the floating opera on the Grand Canal at sundown.

Two pigeons watched them as they drifted away.

"Who *was* that **masked duck**?" said one pigeon to the other. "Should we have had our pictures taken with him?"

"Naw," said the other pigeon. "He's probably just another crazy tourist who likes to wear weird outfits."

Word List

awkwardly (AWK·ward·lee): In a clumsy way; not gracefully

awning (AWE·ning): A piece of canvas material placed over a door or window that keeps out sun or rain

canal (kah·NAL): A waterway built by engineers for travel by boats or ships

dedicated (DED·i·kay·ted): Devoted or loyal to a person, purpose, or course of action

dungeon (DUN·jin): A dark underground jail, especially in a castle

gondola (GAHN·duh·la): A long, narrow boat with curved ends and a flat bottom

gondoliers (ghan·duh·LEERS): The people who control a gondola, usually with an oar or pole

jolt (JOLT): A sudden, rough movement

palette (PAL·it): A thin, oval board with a hole for the thumb that is used by a painter to mix colors

protested (pro·TES·ted):
Complained strongly; showed
much disagreement

scenic (SEE·nick): Relating to
natural or beautiful scenery

signora (sin·YOUR·a): An Italian
word used for Mrs. or madam

Questions

1. Did you suspect anyone else besides El Ducko of stealing the priceless painting from the Doge's Palace?
2. If you were a famous artist, what would your name be?
3. What did Miss Mallard discover about the drawing numbered 1496 that disturbed her?
4. Why was Gino traveling so slowly through the canals?

Did he mean it when he kept saying "Pronto, signora"?

5. Have you ever been to a museum? Do you have a favorite painting or work of art?

Acknowledgments

My thanks and appreciation go to Jon Anderson, president and publisher of Simon & Schuster Children's Books, and his talented team: Karen Nagel, executive editor; Karin Paprocki, art director; Tiara Iandiorio, designer; Elizabeth Mims, managing editor; Bernadette Flinn, production manager; Tricia Lin, assistant editor; and Richard Ackoon, executive coordinator; for launching out into the world again these incredible new editions of my Miss Mallard Mystery books for today's young readers everywhere.

FAST·FUN·READS

LOOKING FOR A FAST, FUN READ?
BE SURE TO MAKE IT ALADDIN QUIX!